oo
V
w
Oo
v
Z
z
W
ng
Ng
Zainab and Viv
sit on swings.

Zainab swings up and jumps off.

Viv swings up...

...twists and slips!

Viv's foot is red and sore.

Zainab tells Dad.
Viv is weeping.

Viv, Zainab, and Dad
wait in a hospital waiting room.

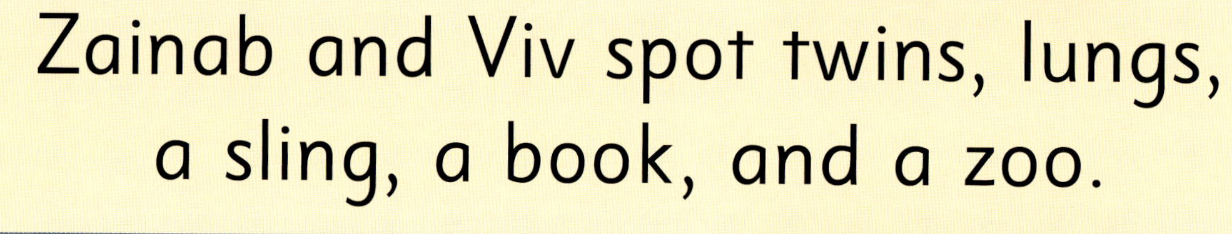

Zainab and Viv spot twins, lungs, a sling, a book, and a zoo.

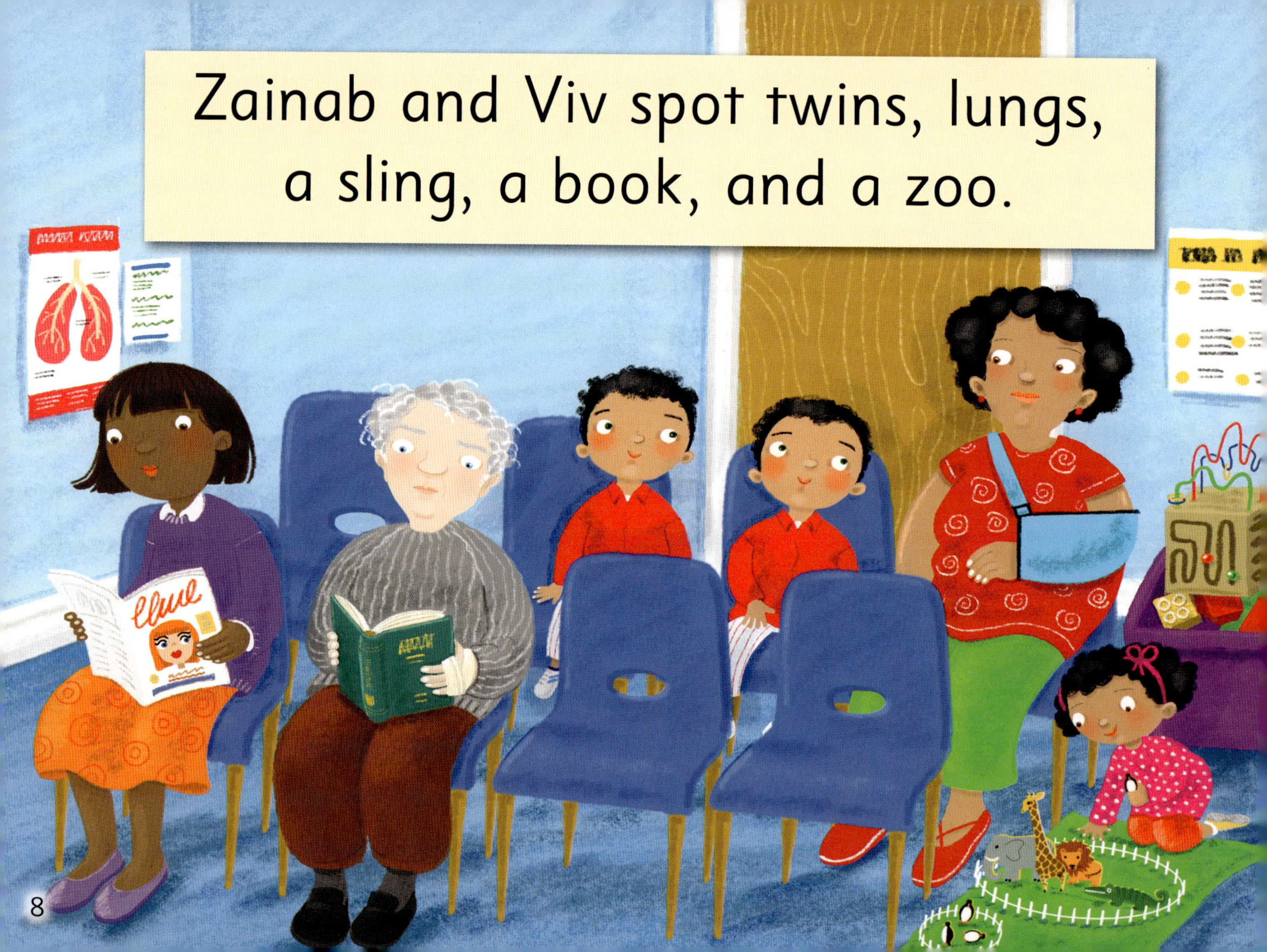

In Room Seven,
Doctor Bloom looks at Viv's foot.

Viv's foot
is sprained.

Doctor Bloom dresses Viv's foot.

Viv will feel well again soon.